Doodle
and Draw
Inside,
Outside,
Everywhere

W9-CHX-380

This edition published by Parragon Books Ltd in 2014 and distributed by

Parragon Inc.
440 Park Avenue South, 13th Floor
New York, NY 10016
www.parragon.com

Copyright © Parragon Books Ltd 2014

Written by Susan Fairbrother   Illustrated by Bella Bee

All rights reserved. No part of this publication may be reproduced, stored in a retrieval
system or transmitted, in any form or by any means, electronic, mechanical, photocopying,
recording or otherwise, without the prior permission of the copyright holder.

ISBN 978-1-4723-6496-8

Printed in China

Doodle
and Draw
Inside,
Outside,
Everywhere

Add bunny passengers to the train.

Doodle something for Mouse to pull.

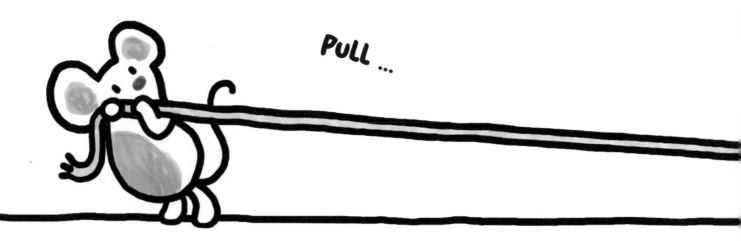

PULL ...

Doodle something for Mouse to push.

PUSH ...

Happy

Sad

Triangles could be ...

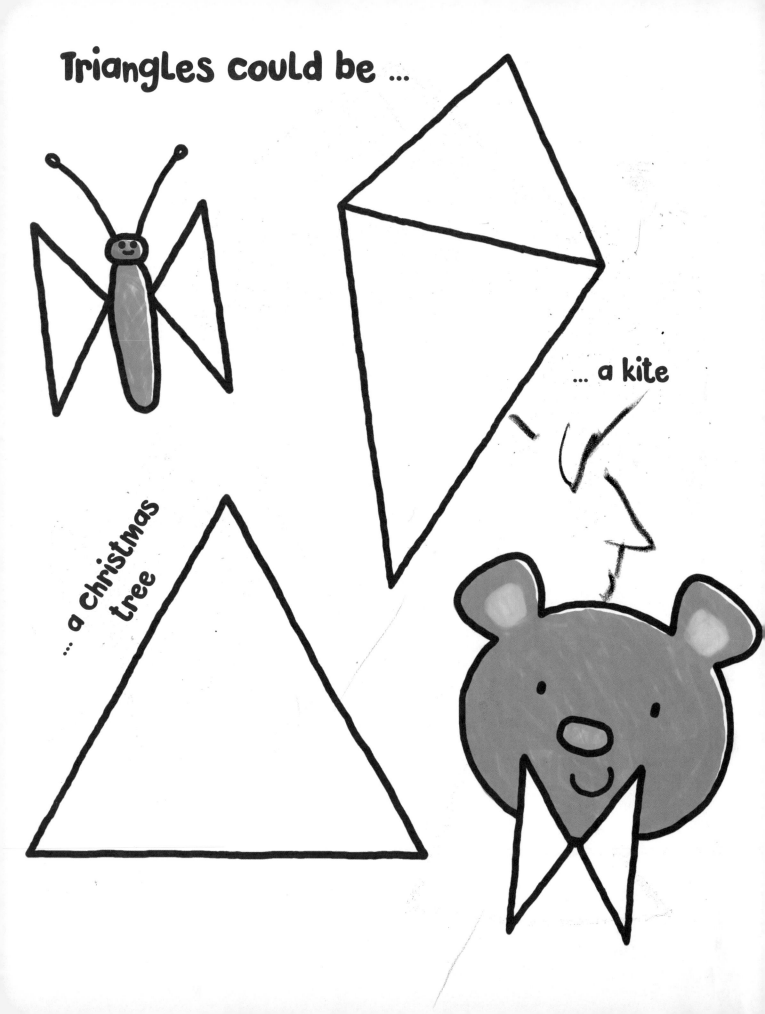

... a kite

... a christmas tree

Triangles have three sides.
Draw more triangle pictures.

Add 3 flags to
the palace.

A fairy tale needs a prince
and a princess. Add them here.

Scary!
Add more spiders
with 8 legs.

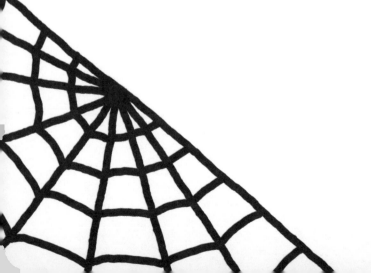

Doodle more LONG snakes and more SHORT snakes.

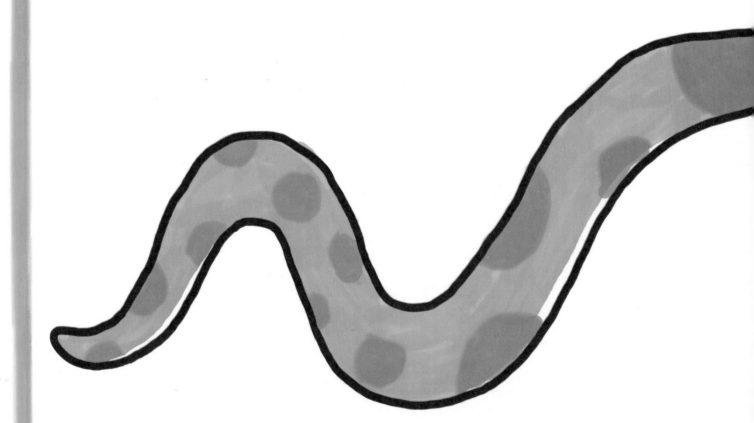

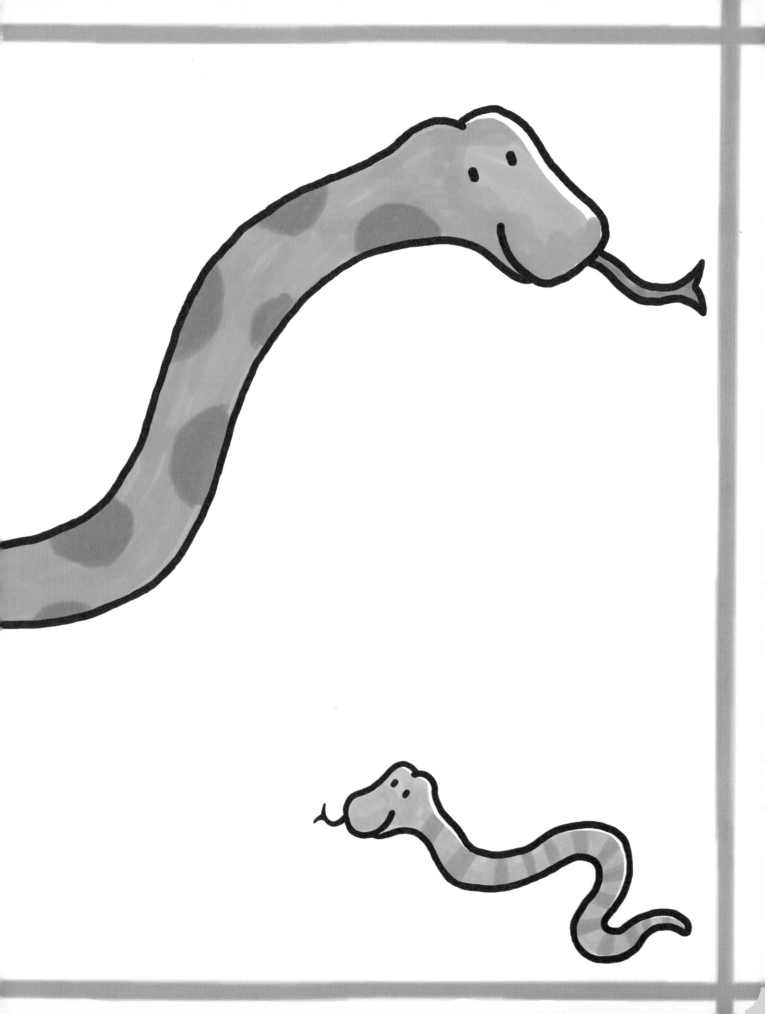

Draw more animals climbing UP the hill and some whizzing DOWN.

FULL

EMPTY

Fill up the empty milkshake glasses!

Add more birds ABOVE the water.

Doodle more
fish BELOW
the waves.

The treasure map has been LOST.
Doodle a new one.

The treasure has been FOUND!
Add more coins to the chest.

squares could be ...

... a present

... a robot

squares have 4 sides.
Draw more square pictures!

Add 3 more apples to the tree.

Doodle 2 more butterfly friends.

Moo!

Draw 1 more cow on the hill.

Triangle spikes!

Add triangles to every dinosaur to make them all really spiky.

RAINY

Give each bear a colorful umbrella.

SUNNY

Give all the cats
sunglasses.

Draw yourself in the mirror.

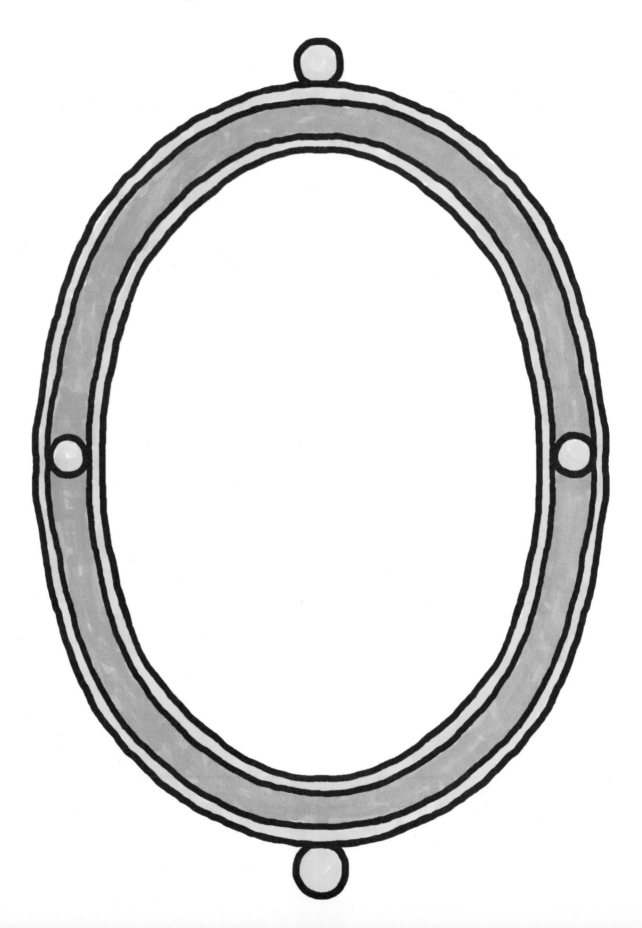

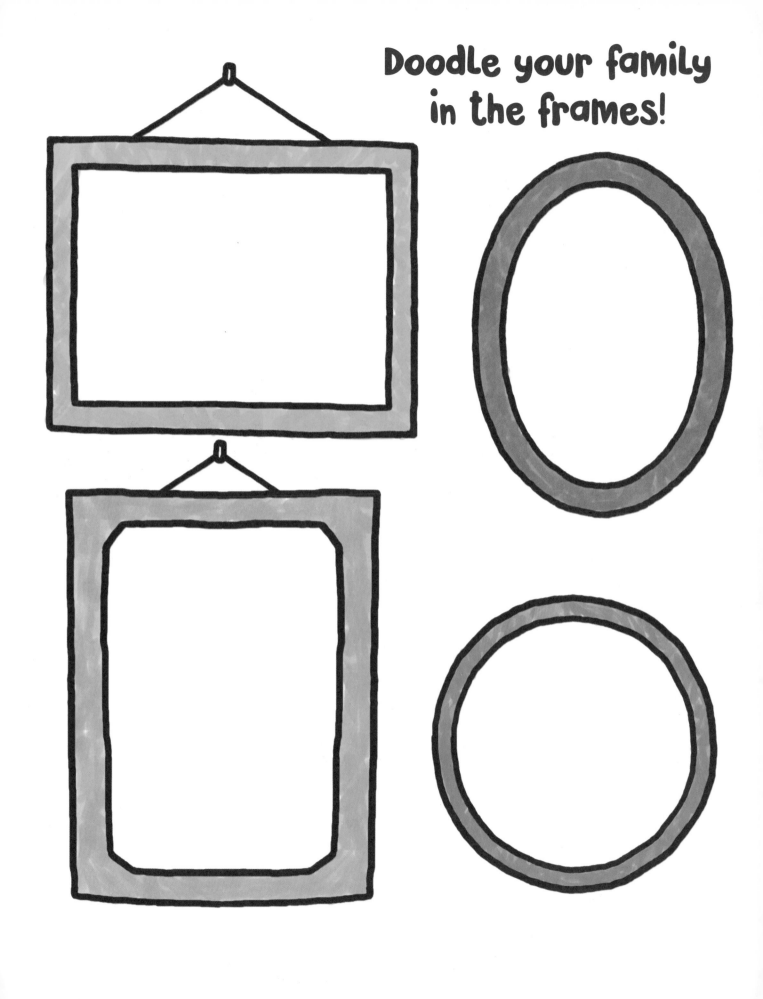

Doodle your family in the frames!

Add 3 more cookies to the plate.

Doodle 4 more pieces of fruit.

Draw 2 more chocolate chip cookies.

Add 5 more cupcakes.

Fee fi fo fum!
Draw the rest
of the giant.

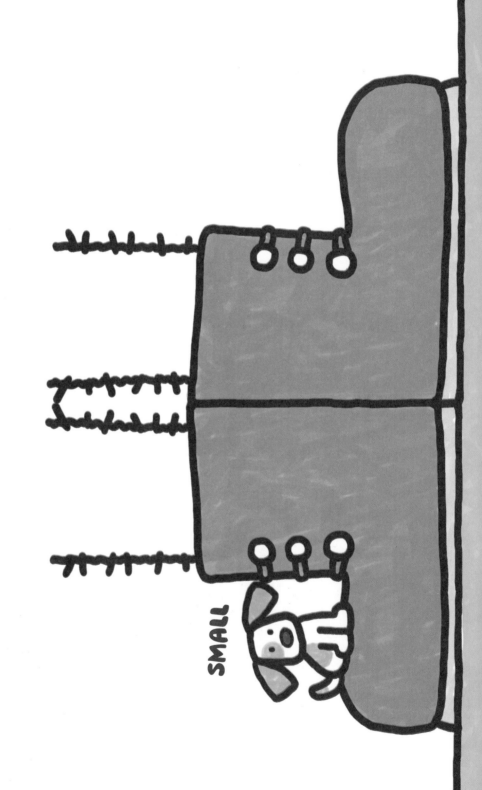

SMALL

Give everyone a new hat!

Bears love picnics!

CIRCLES
Add more apples.

TRIANGLES
Add more pizza slices.

Draw more stars in the sky and owls on the branch.

NIGHT

DAY

Doodle more clouds and little rabbits!

Who lives in the castle?

Ready to race? Doodle more cars on the track.

DOWN

Have you seen my friends?
Doodle lots more penguins on the ice.

Draw a house for the mouse.

Draw a hat for the cat.

Half pictures! Doodle the other side.

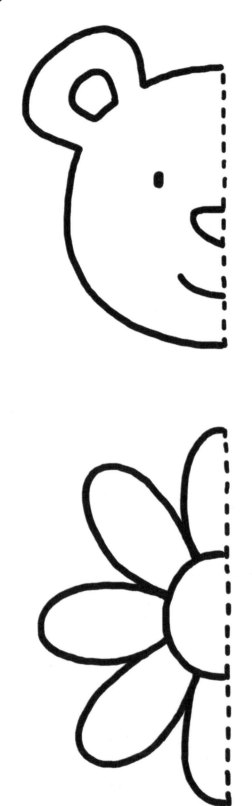

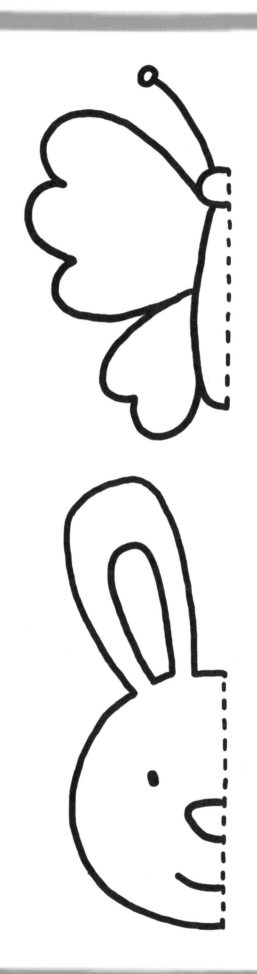

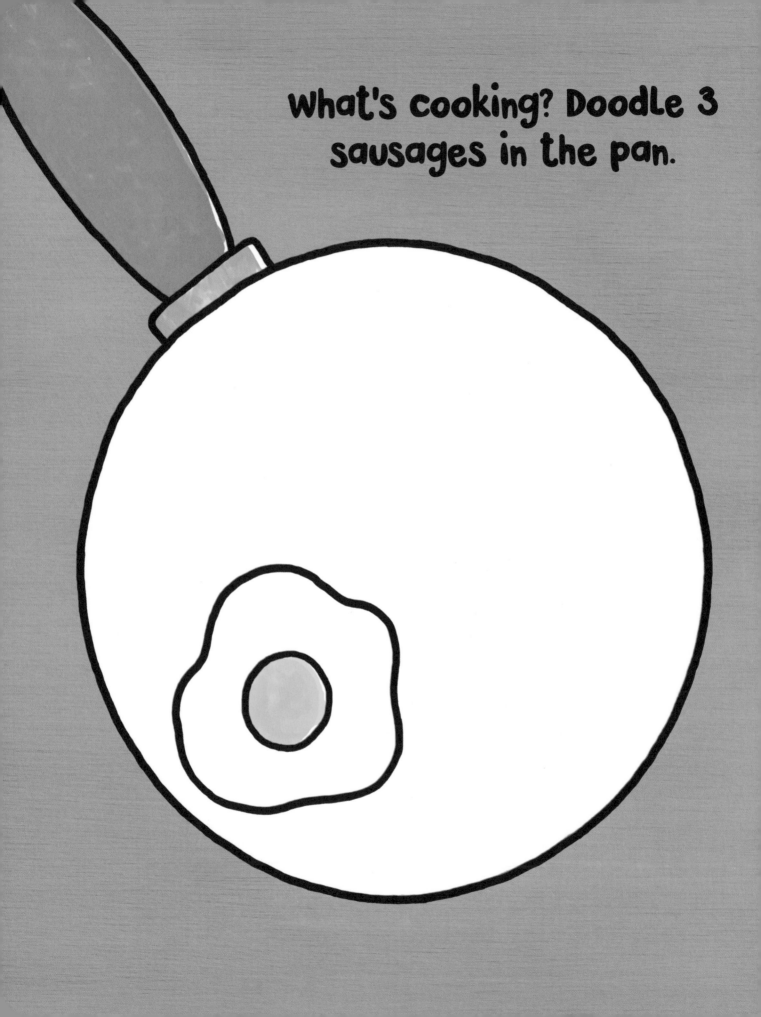

What's cooking? Doodle 3 sausages in the pan.

fill the
page with
circle bubbles!

Complete the city. Draw TALL skyscrapers and SHORT houses.

Doodle lots of tasty popcorn. Who's got the most?

Rabbit

Mouse

Bird

Wow, what a sight! Add purple fireworks.

Add green fireworks here.

Give each monkey
a pair of boots
and a big puddle
to splash in!

Add a red
balloon to
every string.

Pop a fish on the end of each line.

Give everyone a pair of funky glasses!

Draw 2 more colorful kites.

Draw BIG socks and BIG underpants on the clotheslines.

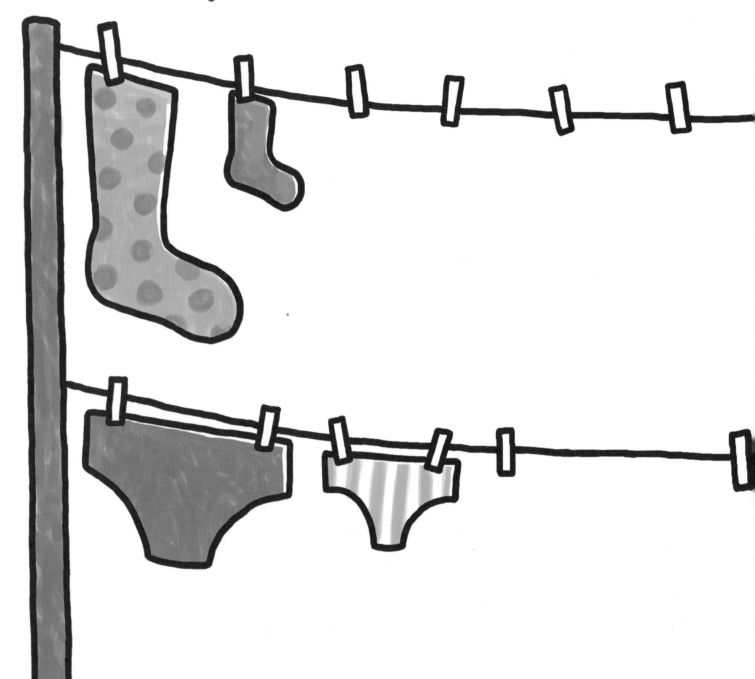

Doodle SMALL socks and SMALL underpants, too!

Draw some zigzag lines.

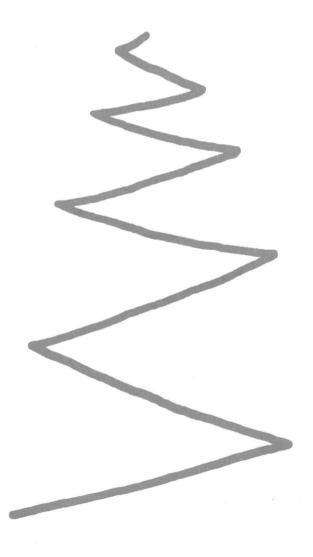

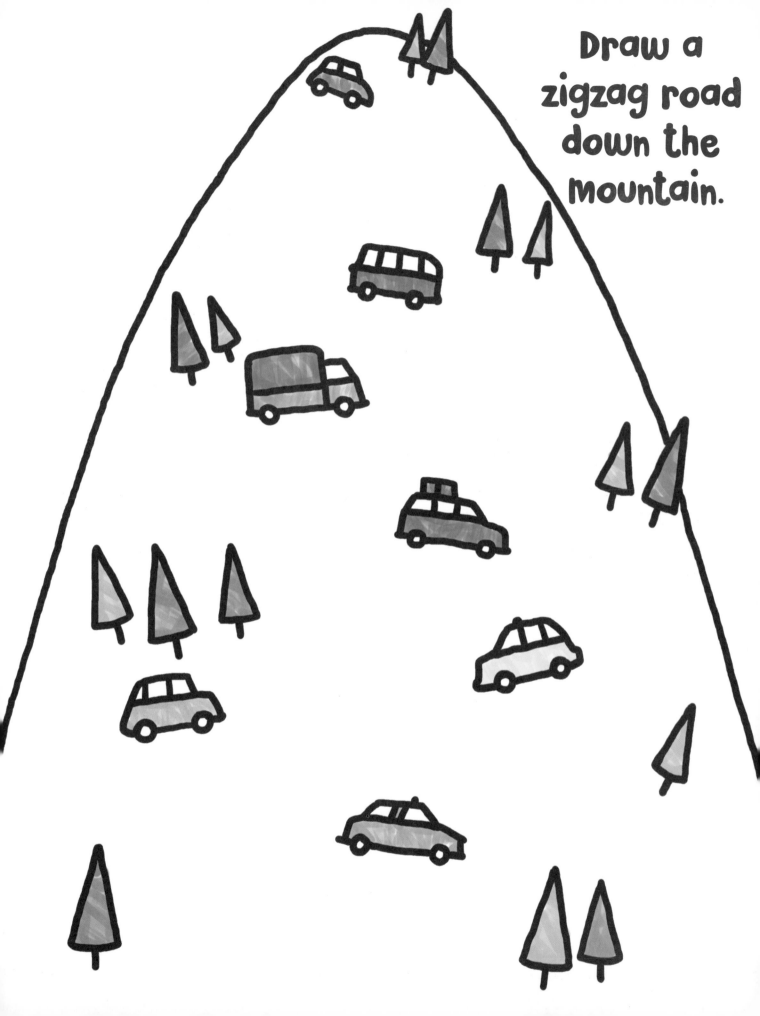

Draw a zigzag road down the mountain.

SPRING

Draw Lots
of Leaves on
the tree.

FALL

Add fallen leaves
in a big pile!

Draw 5 more footprints on each trail.

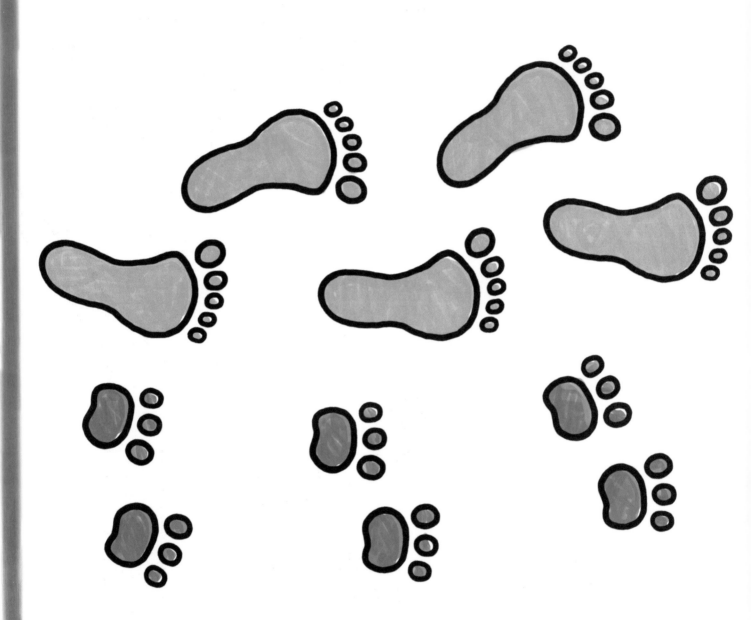

Doodle 2 rabbits in each warren.

Draw a wig for the pig.

Draw a dog on the log.

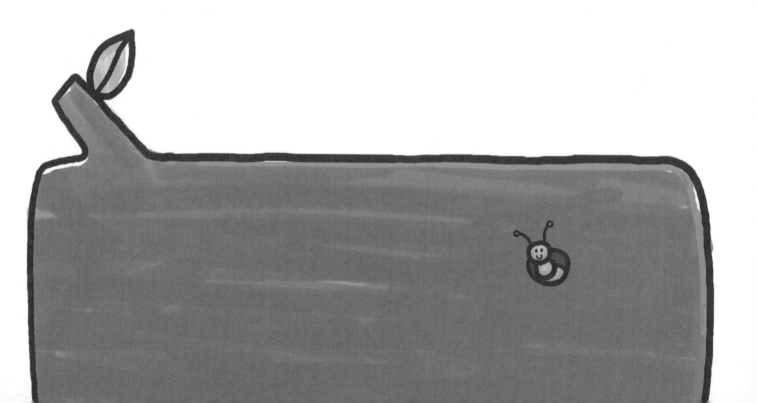

Feathery friends. Draw some more!

How many birds
did you doodle?

Complete the pizzas with more triangle slices.

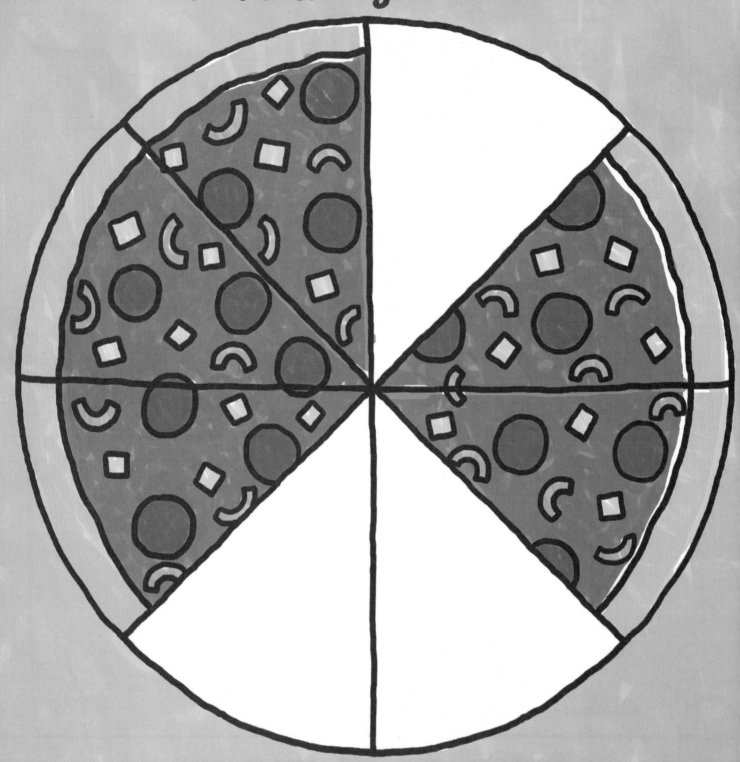

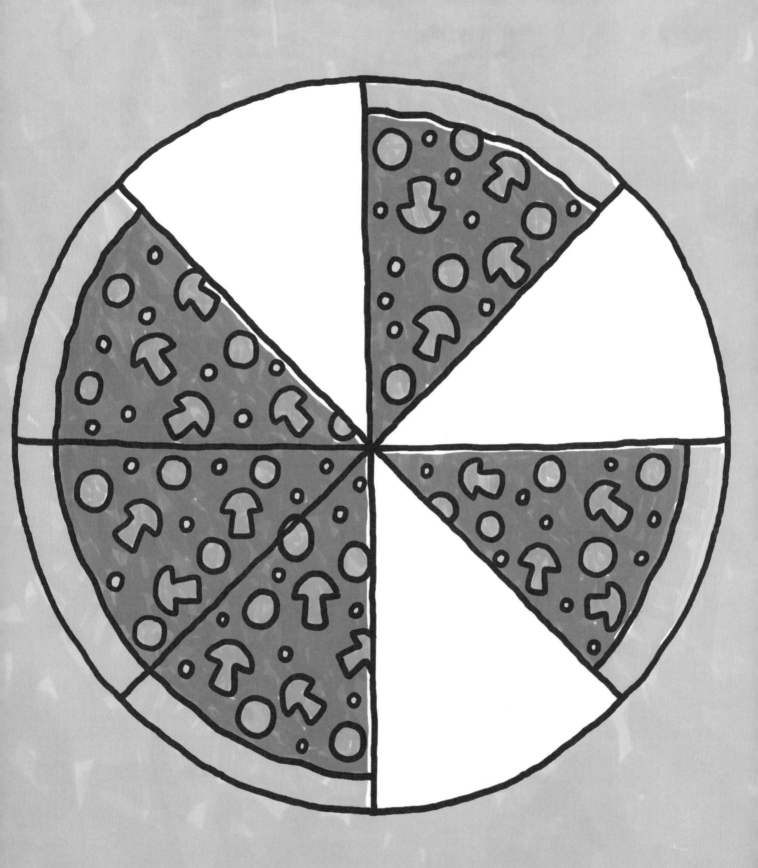

Who's on the seesaw?

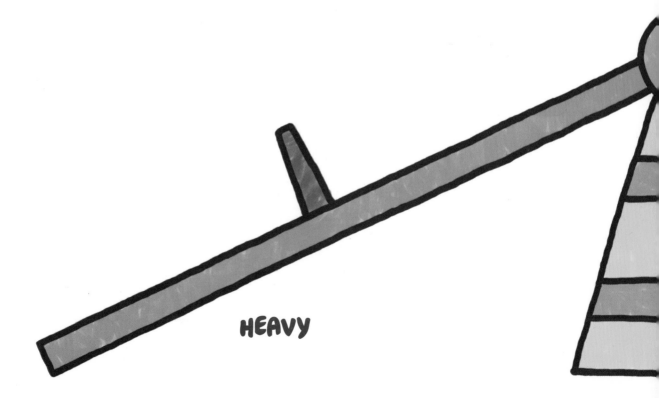

HEAVY

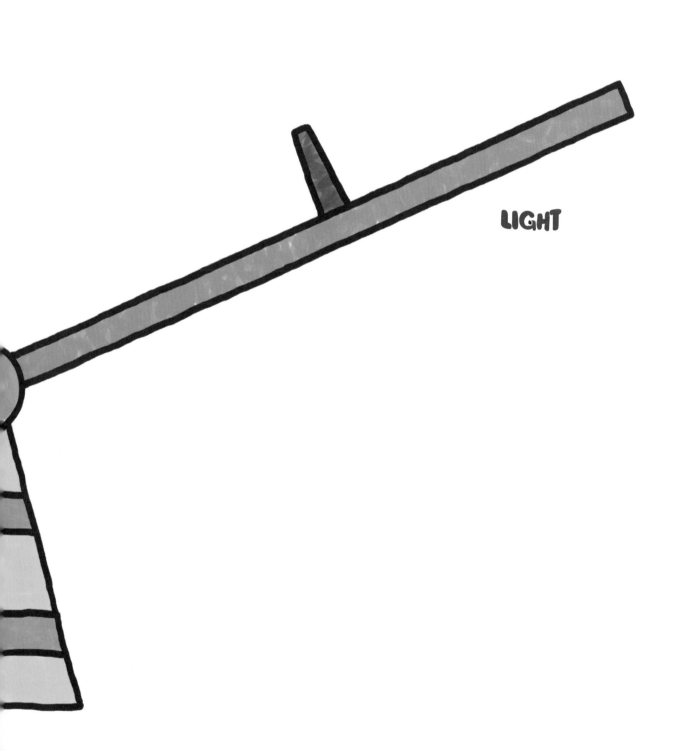

LIGHT

Draw SomeonE INSIDE.

DRAW SOMEONE OUTSIDE.

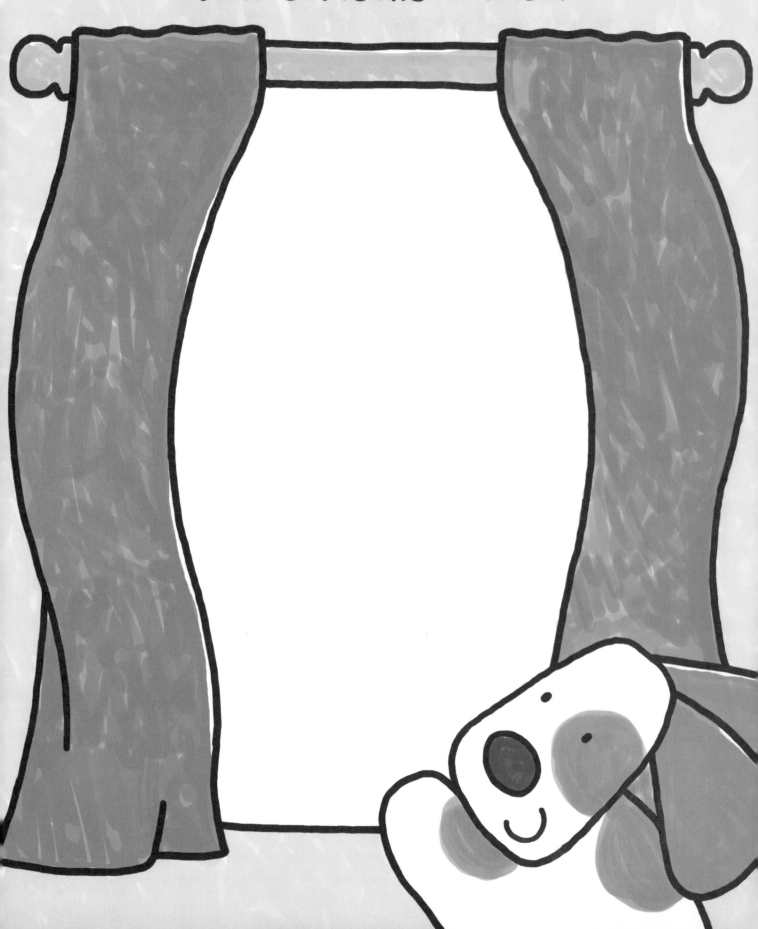

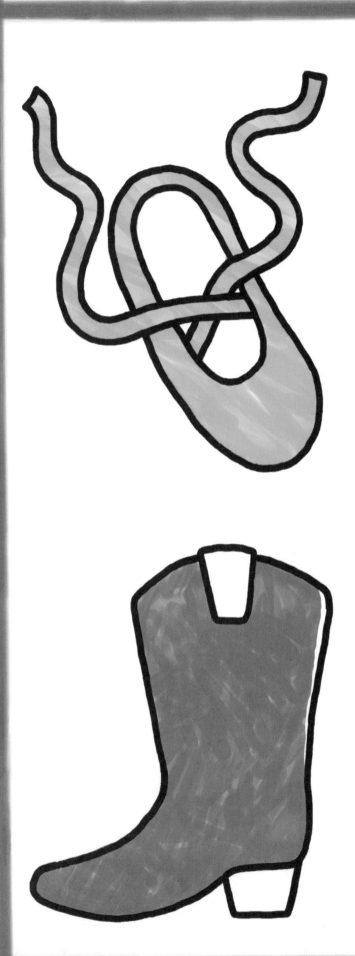

Doodle the
missing shoes to
make 4 pairs.

Doodle more cats up at the top.

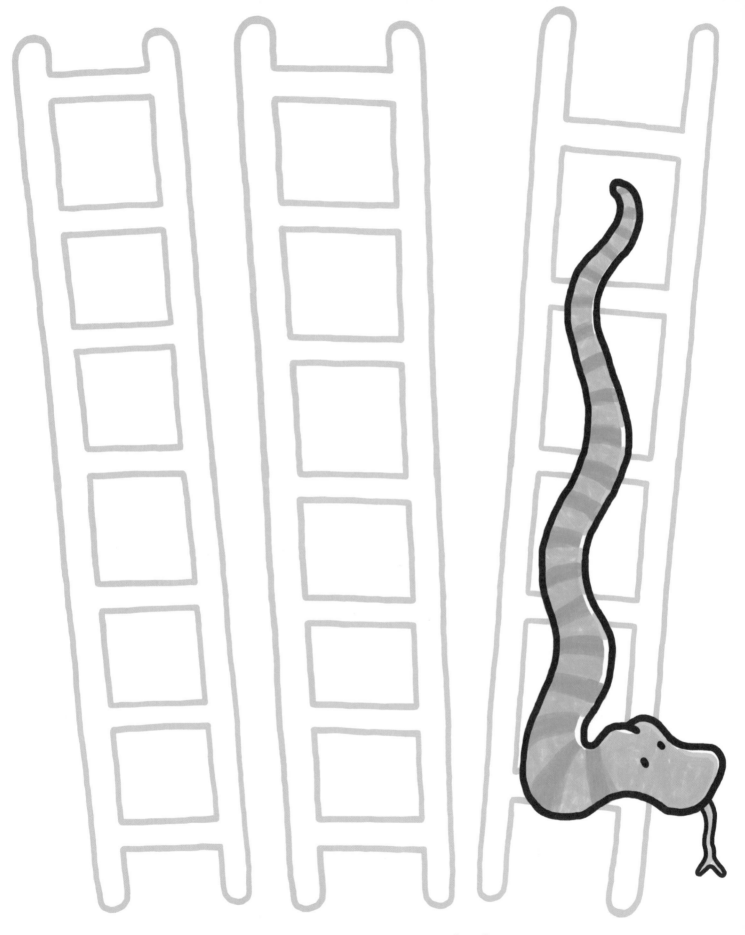

Draw more snakes sliding DOWN.

Who's going OVER this bridge?

Trip, trap, trip, trap!

Who's UNDER this bridge?

Monkeys have LONG tails.
Draw them in.

Hedgehog has
SHORT spikes.
Add lots more.

sad snowman! Doodle him a friend.

Happy Snowman! Draw another.

Add 5 more circles to finish this one.

Add 4 more circles on this one!

Add 4 circles to finish this caterpillar.

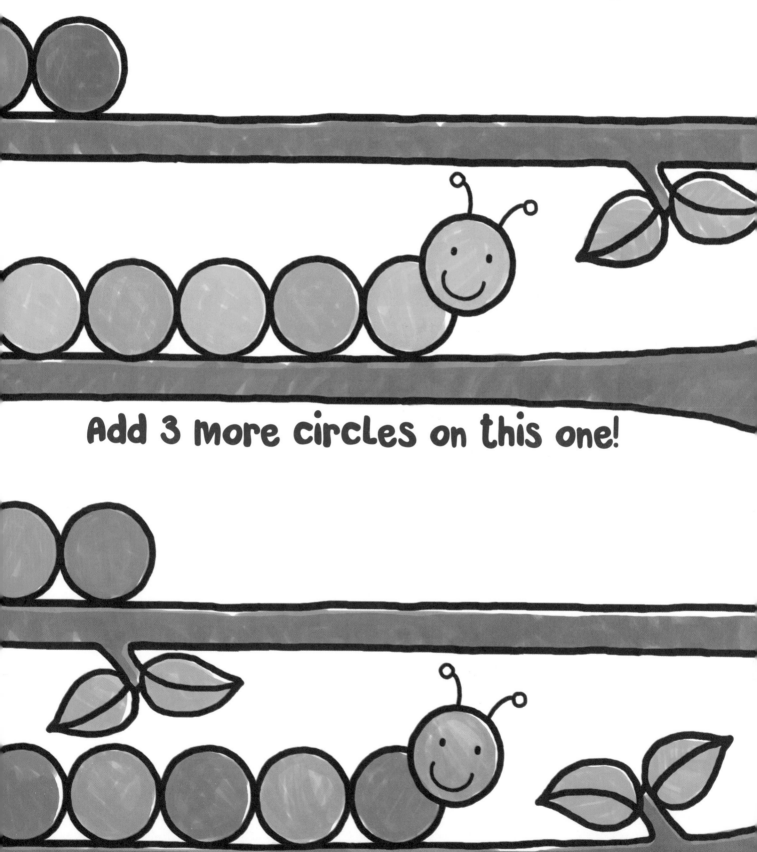

Add 3 more circles on this one!

Add a big sail to the ship.

Draw a pirate in
each porthole.

Doodle more water to make the plants grow!

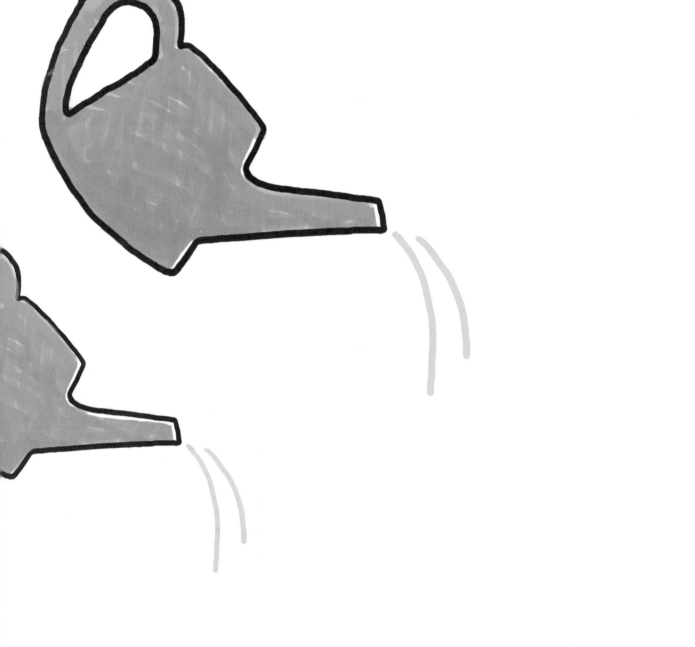

They've grown! Doodle pretty flowers.

Doodle a door!

CLOSED

who's at the door?

OPEN

circles could be ...

... a ball

... a pizza

circles have no corners.
Draw more circle pictures!

Draw 3 more passengers on the ferris wheel.

scribble some sea creatures!